The Owl Who Was Afraid of the Dark

Plop was a baby Barn Owl, and he lived with his Mummy and Daddy at the top of a very tall tree in a field. He was exactly the same as every baby Barn Owl that has ever been – except for one thing.

Plop was afraid of the dark.

The Cat Who Wanted to Go Home

Suzy is a little striped cat who lives in a French seaside village with a fisherman and his four sons. One day she climbs into the basket of a balloon and gets carried over the Channel to an English seaside village. But Suzy is determined to get back home . . .

Also by Jill Tomlinson

The Aardvark Who Wasn't Sure
The Gorilla Who Wanted to Grow Up
The Hen Who Wouldn't Give Up
The Otter Who Wanted to Know
Penguin's Progress

Jill Tomlinson

The Owl Who Was Afraid of the Dark

The Cat Who Wanted to Go Home

Illustrated by Susan Hellard

First published in Great Britain as two separate volumes:

The Owl Who Was Afraid of the Dark
First published in Great Britain 1968
by Methuen & Co Ltd
Published 1992 by Mammoth
Text copyright © 1968 The Estate of Jill Tomlinson
Illustrations copyright © 1991 Susan Hellard

The Cat Who Wanted to Go Home
First published in Great Britain 1972
by Methuen Children's Books Ltd
New edition published 1992 by Mammoth
Text copyright © 1972 The Estate of Jill Tomlinson
Illustrations copyright © 1991 Susan Hellard

This omnibus edition first published 1994 by Mammoth
Reissued 1997 by Mammoth
an imprint of Reed International Books Limited
Michelin House, 81 Fulham Road, London SW3 6RB

ISBN 0 7497 1965 6

10 9 8 7 6 5 4 3 2

A CIP catalogue record for this title
is available from the British Library

Printed and bound in Great Britain
by Cox & Wyman Ltd, Reading, Berkshire

CONTENTS

The Owl Who Was Afraid of the Dark

The Cat Who Wanted to Go Home

The Owl who was Afraid of the Dark

DARK IS EXCITING

Plop was a baby Barn Owl, and he lived with his Mummy and Daddy at the top of a very tall tree in a field.

Plop was fat and fluffy.

He had a beautiful heart-shaped ruff.

He had enormous, round eyes.

He had very knackety knees.

In fact he was exactly the same as every baby Barn Owl that has ever been – except for one thing.

Plop was afraid of the dark.

"You *can't* be afraid of the dark,"

6

said his Mummy. "Owls are *never* afraid of the dark."

"This one is," Plop said.

"But owls are *night* birds," she said.

Plop looked down at his toes. "I don't want to be a night bird," he mumbled. "I want to be a day bird."

"You *are* what you *are*," said Mrs Barn Owl firmly.

"Yes, I know," agreed Plop, "and what I are is afraid of the dark."

"Oh dear," said Mrs Barn Owl. It was clear that she was going to need a lot of patience. She shut her eyes and tried to think how best she could help Plop not to be afraid. Plop waited.

His mother opened her eyes again. "Plop, you are only afraid of the dark because you don't know about it. What *do* you know about the dark?"

"It's black," said Plop.

7

"Well, that's wrong for a start. It can be silver or blue or grey or lots of other colours, but almost never black. What else do you know about it?"

"I don't like it," said Plop. "I do not like it AT ALL."

"That's not *knowing* something," said his mother. "That's *feeling* something. I don't think you know anything about the dark at all."

"Dark is nasty," Plop said loudly.

"You don't know that. You have never had your beak outside the nest-hole after dusk. I think you had better go down into the world and find out a lot more about the dark before you make up your mind about it."

"Now?" said Plop.

"Now," said his mother.

Plop climbed out of the nest-hole and wobbled along the branch outside. He peeped over the edge. The world seemed to be a very long way down.

"I'm not a very good lander," he said. "I might spill myself."

"Your landing will improve with practice," said his mother. "Look! There's a little boy down there on the edge of the wood collecting sticks. Go and talk to him about it."

"Now?" said Plop.

"Now," said his mother. So Plop shut his eyes, took a deep breath, and fell off his branch.

His small white wings carried him down, but, as he said, he was not a good lander. He did seven very fast somersaults past the little boy.

"Ooh!" cried the little boy. "A giant Catherine-wheel!"

9

"Actually," said the Catherine-wheel, picking himself up, "I'm a Barn Owl."

"Oh yes – so you are," said the little boy with obvious disappointment. "Of course, you couldn't be a firework yet. Dad says we can't have the fireworks until it gets dark. Oh, I wish it would hurry up and get dark *soon*."

"You *want* it to get dark?" said Plop in amazement.

"Oh, YES," said the little boy. "DARK IS EXCITING. And tonight is specially exciting because we're going to have fireworks."

"What are fireworks?" asked Plop. "I don't think owls have them – not Barn Owls, anyway."

"Don't you?" said the little boy. "Oh, you poor thing. Well, there are rockets, and flying saucers, and volcanoes, and

10

golden rain, and sparklers, and . . ."

"But what *are* they?" begged Plop. "Do you eat them?"

"NO!" laughed the little boy. "Daddy sets fire to their tails and they *whoosh* into the air and fill the sky with coloured stars – well, the rockets, that is. I'm allowed to hold the sparklers."

"What about the volcanoes? And the golden rain? What do they do?"

"Oh, they sort of burst into showers of stars. The golden rain *pours* – well, like rain."

"And the flying saucers?"

"Oh, they're super! They whizz round your head and make a sort of *wheeee* noise. I like them best."

"I think I would like fireworks," said Plop.

"I'm sure you would," the little boy said. "Look here, where do you live?"

11

"Up in that tree – in the top flat. There are squirrels farther down."

"That big tree in the middle of the field? Well, you can watch our fireworks from there! That's our garden – the one with the swing. You look out as soon as it gets dark . . ."

"Does it *have* to be dark?" asked Plop.

"Of course it does! You can't see fireworks unless it's dark. Well, I must go. These sticks are for the bonfire."

"Bonfire?" said Plop. "What's that?"

"You'll see if you look out tonight. Goodbye!"

"Goodbye," said Plop, bobbing up and down in a funny little bow.

He watched the boy run across the field, and then took a little run himself, spread his wings, and fluttered up to the landing branch. He slithered along

it on his tummy and dived head first into the nest-hole.

"Well?" said his mother.

"The little boy says DARK IS EXCITING."

"And what do you think, Plop?"

"I still do not like it AT ALL," said Plop, "but I'm going to watch the fireworks – if you will sit by me."

"I will sit by you," said his mother.

"So will I," said his father, who had just woken up. "I like fireworks."

So that is what they did.

When it began to get dark, Plop waddled to the mouth of the nest-hole and peered out cautiously.

"Come on, Plop! I think they're starting," called Mr Barn Owl. He was already in position on a big branch at the very top of the tree. "We shall see beautifully from here."

Plop took two brave little steps out of the nest-hole.

"I'm here," said his mother quietly. "Come on."

So together, wings almost touching, they flew up to join Mr Barn Owl.

14

They were only just in time. There were flames leaping and crackling at the end of the little boy's garden. "That must be the bonfire!" squeaked Plop.

Hardly had Plop got his wings tucked away, when "*WHOOSH!*" – up went a rocket and spat out a shower of green stars. "Ooooh!" said Plop, his eyes like saucers.

A fountain of dancing stars sprang up from the ground – and another and another. "Ooooh!" said Plop again.

"You sound like a Tawny owl," said his father. "Goodness! What's that?"

Something was whizzing about leaving bright trails of squiggles behind it and making a loud "Wheeee!" noise.

"Oh, that's a flying saucer," said Plop.

"Really?" his father said. "I've never

seen one of those before. You seem to know all about it. What's that fizzy one that keeps jigging up and down?"

"I expect that's my friend with a sparkler. Oooooh! There's a me!"

"I beg your pardon?" said Plop's father.

"It's a Catherine-wheel! The little boy thought I was a Catherine-wheel when I landed. Oh, isn't it beautiful? And he thought *I* was one!"

Mr Barn Owl watched the whirling, sparking circles spinning round and round.

"That must have been quite a landing!" he said.

DARK IS KIND

When the very last firework had faded away, Mr Barn Owl turned to Plop.

"Well, son," he said. "I'm off hunting now. Would you like to come?"

Plop looked at the darkness all around them. It seemed even blacker after the bright fireworks. "Er – not this time, thank you, Daddy. I can't see; I've got stars in my eyes."

"I see," said his father. "In that case I shall have to go by myself." He floated off into the darkness like a great white moth.

Plop turned in distress to his mother.

"I *wanted* to go with him. I *want* to like the dark. It's just that I don't seem to be able to."

"You will be able to, Plop. I'm quite sure about that."

"I'm not sure," said Plop.

"Well, I *am*," his mother said. "Now, come on. You'd better have your rest. You were awake half the day."

So Plop had his midnight rest, and when he woke up, his father was back with his dinner. Plop swallowed it in one huge gulp. "That was nice," he said. "What was it?"

"A mouse," said Mr Barn Owl.

"I like mouse," said Plop. "What's next?"

"I have no idea," his father said. "It's Mummy's turn now. You'll have to wait till she gets back."

Plop was always hungry, and his mother and father were kept very busy bringing him food all night long. When daylight came, they were very tired and just wanted to go to sleep.

"Bedtime, Plop," said Mrs Barn Owl.

"I don't want to go to bed," said Plop. "I want to be a day bird."

"Well, *I* am a night bird," said his mother. "And if your father and I don't get any sleep today, *you* won't get anything to eat tonight."

Plop did not like the sound of that at all, so he drew himself up straight and tall – well, as tall as he could – and tried to go to sleep.

He did sleep for half the morning, but then he woke up full of beans – or perhaps it was mouse – and he just could not go back to sleep again.

He jiggled up and down on the

branch where his poor parents were trying to roost. He practised standing on one leg, and taking off, and landing, and other important things that a little owl has to learn to do. Then he thought he would try out his voice. He tried to make a real, grown-up Barn Owl noise.

"EEeek!" he screeched. "EEEEEK!"

It sounded like the noise a cat makes if you accidentally tread upon its tail. Plop was very pleased with it.

Mrs Barn Owl was not. She half opened one bleary eye. "Plop, dear," she said. "Wouldn't you like to go down into the world again and find out some more about the dark?"

"Now?" said Plop.

"Now," said his mother.

"Don't you want to hear my screech first? It's getting jolly good."

"I heard it," Mrs Barn Owl said

"Look, there's an old lady in a deck-chair down there in that garden. Go and disturb – I mean, go and find out what she thinks about the dark."

So Plop shut his eyes, took a deep breath, and fell off his branch.

He did not get his wings working in time. He fell faster and faster and finally plunged at the old lady's feet with an earth-shaking thump.

"Gracious!" cried the old lady. "A thunderbolt!"

"A-a-a-actually, I'm a Barn Owl," said the thunderbolt when he had got his breath back.

"Really?" said the old lady, peering at Plop over the top of her glasses. "I do beg your pardon. My eyes are not as good as they used to be. How nice of you to – er – drop in."

"Well, it wasn't nice of me, exactly," Plop said truthfully. "I came to ask you about something."

"Did you?" said the old lady. "Now what could that be, I wonder?"

"I wanted to ask you about the dark. You see, I'm a bit afraid of it, and that's rather awkward for an owl. We're supposed to be night birds."

"That is a problem," said the old lady. "Have you tried carrots?"

"What?"

"Don't say 'what', say 'I beg your pardon' if you don't hear the first time. I said, have you tried carrots? Wonderful things, carrots."

"I don't think owls have carrots – not Barn Owls, anyway."

"Oh. A pity. I've always sworn by carrots for helping one to see in the dark."

"I *can* see in the dark," said Plop. "I can see for miles and miles."

"Now, don't boast. It is not nice for little boys' to boast." The old lady leaned forward and peered closely at Plop. "I suppose you are a little boy? It's so difficult to tell, these days. They all look the same."

"Yes," said Plop. "I'm a boy owl, and

23

I want to go hunting with Daddy, but he always goes hunting in the dark, and I'm afraid of it."

"How very odd," said the old lady. "Now, I love the dark. I expect you will when you are my age. DARK IS KIND."

"Tell me," Plop said.

"*Please*," said the old lady. "Such a little word, but it works wonders."

"Tell me, please," said Plop obediently.

"Well, now," the old lady began. "Dark is kind in all sorts of ways. Dark hides things – like shabby furniture and the hole in the carpet. It hides my wrinkles and my gnarled old hands. I can forget that I'm old in the dark."

"I don't think owls get wrinkles," said Plop. "Not Barn Owls, anyway. They just get a bit moth-eaten looking."

24

"Don't interrupt!" said the old lady. "It is very rude to interrupt. Where was I? Yes – dark is kind when you are old. I can sit in the dark and *remember*. I remember my dear husband, and my children when they were small, and all the good times we had together. I am never lonely in the dark."

"I haven't much to remember, yet," said Plop. "I'm rather new, you see."

"Dark is quiet, too," said the old lady, looking hard at Plop. "Dark is restful – unlike a little owl I know."

"Me?" said Plop.

"You," said the old lady. "When I was a little girl, children were seen but not heard."

"I'm not children," said Plop. "I'm a Barn Owl."

"Same thing," said the old lady. "You remind me very much of my son

William when he was about four. He had the same knackety knees."

"Are my knees knackety?" asked Plop, squinting downwards. "I can't see them. My tummy gets in the way."

"Very," said the old lady, "but I expect they'll straighten out in time. William's did. Now, I'm going indoors to have a little rest."

Plop was surprised. "I thought it was only owls who slept in the daytime," he said. "Are you a night bird, too?"

The old lady smiled. "No, just an old bird. A very tired old bird."

"Goodbye, then. I'll go now," said Plop. "Thank you for telling me about the dark."

He fluttered up to the old lady's shoulder and nibbled her ear very gently.

The old lady was enchanted. "An

owl kiss!" she said. "How very kind."

Plop jumped down again and bobbed his funny little bow.

"Such charming manners!" said the old lady.

Then Plop took a little run, spread

his wings, and flew up to the landing branch.

"Well?" said his mother.

"The old lady says DARK IS KIND."

"And what do you think, Plop?"

"I still do not like it AT ALL. Do you think my knees are knackety?"

"Of course," said his mother. "All little Barn Owls have knackety knees."

"Oh, good," said Plop. "And what do you think the old lady said? She said children should be seen but not heard!"

Mr Barn Owl opened one sleepy eye:

"Hear! Hear!" he said.

DARK IS FUN

That evening when it was getting dark, Mr Barn Owl invited Plop to go hunting with him again. "Coming, son?" he said. "It's a lovely night."

"Er – not this time, thank you, Daddy," said Plop, who was sitting just outside the nest-hole. "I'm busy."

"You don't look busy," Mr Barn Owl said. "What are you doing?"

"I am busy *remembering*," said Plop.

"I see," said his father. "In that case

I shall have to go by myself." He swooped off into the darkness like a great, silent jet aeroplane.

"What are you remembering, Plop?" asked his mother.

"I'm remembering what the old lady said about dark being kind. She says she is never lonely in the dark because she has so much to remember."

"Well then," said Mrs Barn Owl, "this would seem to be a good moment for me to slip out and do a little hunting."

"You're not going to leave me by myself!" said Plop.

"I shan't be very long. I'll try to bring you back something nice."

"But I shall be lonely."

"No, you won't. You just keep busy remembering like the old lady said."

Plop watched his mother float off into the darkness like a white feather.

The darkness seemed to come towards him and wrap itself around him.

"Dark is kind," Plop muttered to himself. "Dark is kind. Oh dear, what shall I remember?" He closed his eyes and tried to remember something to remember. Fireworks! He would remember the fireworks. He had enjoyed them. The darkness had been spotted and striped and sploshed with coloured lights above the glow of the bonfire. He still had stars in his eyes when he thought of it.

Shouts – happy shouts – from under his tree brought Plop back from his remembering. He opened his eyes and peered down through the leaves. There were people running about in his field, and flames were flickering from a pile of sticks. Another bonfire! Did that mean more fireworks?

Plop watched excitedly. He could see now that the people running about were boys – quite big boys in shorts. They were collecting more wood for the fire.

Suddenly they all disappeared into the woods with squeals and yells. All but one, that is. There was one boy left, sitting on a log near the fire.

Plop forgot about being afraid of the dark. He had to know what was going on. So he shut his eyes, took a deep breath, and fell off his branch.

The ground was nearer than he expected it to be, and he landed with an enormous thud.

"Coo!" said the boy on the log. "A roly-poly pudding! Who threw that?"

"Nobody threw me – I just came," said the roly-poly pudding, "and actually I'm a Barn Owl."

"So you are," said the boy. "Have you fallen out of your nest?"

Plop drew himself up as tall as he could. "I did not fall – I flew," he said. "I'm just not a very good lander, that's all. I came to see if you were going to have fireworks, as a matter of fact."

"Fireworks?" said the boy. "No. What made you think that?"

"Well, the bonfire," Plop said.

"Bonfire!" said the boy. "This is no

33

bonfire! This is a camp-fire – and I'm guarding it till the others get back."

"Where have they gone?" asked Plop.

"They've gone to play games in the dark, lucky things."

"Do you *like* playing games in the dark?" asked Plop.

"It's super!" said the boy. "DARK IS FUN. Even quite ordinary games like Hide-and-Seek are fun in the dark. My favourite is the game where one of you stands outside a 'home' with a torch in his hand, and shines it on anything he sees or hears moving. The rest of you have to creep past him and 'home' without being spotted. It's super!"

There was a crash, and a yell of "Scumbo! Got you!" from the wood.

"There – they're playing it now. Old Scumbo always gets caught first. He's got such big feet. You have to creep

34

like a shadow not to be caught. Oh, it *would* be my turn to guard the fire."

"What's the fire for?" asked Plop.

"Well, we cook potatoes in it, and make cocoa, and sing round it."

"What for?"

"What for? Because it's fun, that's why, and because Boy Scouts have always had camp-fires."

"Is that what you are? A Boy Scout?"

"Of course, silly, or I wouldn't be here, would I? I must put some more wood on the fire."

Plop watched the Boy Scout build up the fire. "Could – could I be a Boy Scout, do you think?" he asked.

"I doubt it," said the Scout. "You're a bit on the small side. I suppose you could be a Cub, but you have to be eight years old."

"I'm eight weeks," said Plop.

"Looks as if you'll have a long wait, then, doesn't it?" said the Scout. "Anyway," – he grinned – "you'd look jolly silly in the uniform!"

Plop looked so disappointed that the Scout added, "Never mind. You can stay for the sing-song tonight."

"Oh, can I!" cried Plop. "That would be soo – super!"

"You'd better go home and ask your mother first, though."

So Plop flew up to the nest-hole – and found his mother waiting.

"Where have you been?" she said. She sounded a bit cross, like all mothers when they have been worried.

"I've been talking to a Boy Scout, and he says DARK IS FUN, and he says I can stay for the camp-fire, so can I, Mummy, please?"

"Well, yes, all right," she said.

36

"Oh, super!" said Plop.

So Plop was a Boy Scout for a night. He sat on his new friend's shoulder and was introduced to all the others. They made a great fuss of him and he

had a wonderful time. He did not care for cocoa, but he enjoyed a small potato. His friend blew on it for him to cool it, because he knew that owls swallow their food whole, and a hot potato in the tummy would have been very uncomfortable for Plop!

The Scouts huddled round the fire and sang and sang while the sparks danced. They sang funny songs and sad songs, long songs and short songs. Plop did not sing because he wanted to listen, but every now and then he got a bit excited and fluttered round the boys' heads crying "Eeek! Eeeek!" and everybody laughed.

They sang until the fire had sunk to a deep, red glow and Plop had turned quite pink in its light.

Then it was time to go home, for the boys and for Plop. And when Plop had said goodbye to them all, and bowed and bowed till he ached, he spread his wings and flew up to the landing branch.

"Well?" said his mother.

"I told you. The Boy Scout says DARK IS FUN."

"And what do you think, Plop?"

"I still do not like it AT ALL – but I think camp-fires are super! Did you bring me something special?"

"I did."

Plop swallowed it in one gulp.

"That was nice," he said.

"What was it?"

"A grasshopper."

"I like grass-
hopper," said Plop.
"What's next?"

DARK IS NECESSARY

Plop asked "What's next" a great many times during that night. He sat just outside the nest-hole making loud snoring noises. He was not asleep – just hungry. Owls always snore when they're hungry.

"Oh, Plop. I shall be glad when you can hunt for yourself," said Mrs Barn Owl wearily when Plop had gulped down his seventh – or was it his eighth? – dinner.

"What's next?" asked Plop.

"Nothing," said his mother. "You

can't possibly have room for anything else."

"I have," said Plop. "My mouse place is full up, but my grasshopper place isn't."

"That's just too bad," said Mrs Barn Owl, stretching and settling herself down to roost.

Mr Barn Owl swooped in, clapping his wings. He dropped something at Plop's feet. Plop swallowed it in one gulp. It was deliciously slippery.

"That was nice," he said. "What was it?"

"A fish," said his father.

"I like fish," said Plop. "What's next?"

"Bed," said Mr Barn Owl. He kissed his wife good night – or good day, I suppose it was – and settled himself to roost.

Plop made a few hopeful snoring noises, but it was clear that the feast was over. He wobbled into the nest-hole and was soon fast asleep himself.

It was well into the afternoon when he woke up. He came out on to the landing branch and looked around. His parents were still drawn up as still as carvings, but the squirrels from downstairs were chasing each other up and down the trunk, their tails flying behind them. Plop watched them for a bit. One of them scuttled along the branch just below Plop's and then stopped abruptly and began to wash his face. He did not know that Plop was there – after all, owls are *supposed* to be asleep during the daytime.

Plop could not resist it. He bent down through the leaves and let out his very loudest "Eeeek!"

The squirrel jumped into the air like
a jack-in-a-box, his ears a-quiver and
his eyes like marbles. He flashed down
the trunk and vanished into his hole.

Plop jumped up and down with
delight. But of course he had done it
again: he had woken his mother.

"Plop!"

"Yes, Mummy?"

"Go and find out some more about the dark, please, dear."

"Now?" said Plop.

"Now," said his mother. "Go and ask that little girl what she thinks about it."

"What little girl?"

"That little girl sitting down there – the one with the pony-tail."

"Little girls don't have *tails*."

"This one does. Go on now or you'll miss her."

So Plop shut his eyes, took a deep breath, and fell off his branch.

His landing was a little better than usual. He bounced three times and rolled gently towards the little girl's feet.

"Oh! A woolly ball!" cried the little girl.

"Actually I'm a Barn Owl," said the woolly ball.

"An owl? Are you sure?" she said, putting out a grubby finger and prodding Plop's round fluffy tummy.

"Quite sure," said Plop, backing away and drawing himself up tall.

"Well, there's no need to be huffy," said the little girl. "You bounced. You must expect to be mistaken for a ball if you will go bouncing about the place. I've never met an owl before. Do you say Tu-whit-a-woo?"

"No," said Plop. "That's Tawny Owls."

"Oh, you can't be a proper owl, then," said the little girl. "*Proper* owls say 'Tu-whit-a-woo' !"

"I *am* a proper owl!" said Plop,

getting very cross.
"I am a Barn Owl,
and Barn Owls go
Eeeek like that."

"Oh, don't *do*
that!" said the little
girl, putting her
hands over her ears.

"Well, you shouldn't have made me cross," said Plop. "Anyway – *you* can't be a proper girl."

"*What* did you say?" said the little girl, taking her hands off her ears.

"I said you're not a proper girl. Girls don't have *tails*. Squirrels have tails, rabbits have tails, mice . . ."

"This is a *pony* tail," said the little girl. "It's the longest one in the class," she added proudly.

"But why do you want to look like a pony?" asked Plop.

"Because – oh, because it's the fashion," said the little girl. "Don't you know *anything*?"

"Not much," agreed Plop. "Mummy says that that is why I'm afraid of the dark – because I don't know anything about it. Do *you* like the dark?"

The little girl looked at Plop in surprise. "Well, of course I do," she said. "There has to be dark. DARK IS NECESSARY."

"Dark is nessessess – is whatter?"

"Necessary. We need it. We can't do without it."

"I could do without it," said Plop. "I could do without it very nicely."

"Father Christmas wouldn't come," said the little girl. "You'll have an empty stocking on Christmas day."

"I don't wear stockings," said Plop, "and who is Father Christmas?"

"Well, Father Christmas is a fat, jolly old man with a white beard, and he wears a red suit with a matching hat, and black boots."

"Is that the fashion?" asked Plop.

"No," said the little girl. "It's just what he always wears in pictures of him – although I don't know how anybody knows because nobody has ever seen him."

"What?" said Plop.

"Well, that's what I'm trying to tell you. *Father Christmas only comes in the dark.* He comes in the middle of the night, riding through the sky on a sledge pulled by reindeer."

"Deer?" asked Plop. "In the sky?"

"Magic deer," said the little girl. "Everything about Father Christmas is magic. Otherwise he couldn't possibly get round to all the children in the world in one night – or have enough toys for them all in his sack."

"You didn't tell me about his sack."

"He has a sack full of toys and he puts them in the children's stockings."

"In their stockings?" said Plop. "With their feet in them? There can't be much room – "

"No, silly. We hang empty stockings at the ends of our beds for him to fill. I usually borrow one of Mummy's, but last year I hung up my tights."

"And did he fill them?" breathed Plop.

"No – only one leg, but he did put a sugar mouse in the other one."

"I'd rather have had a real mouse," said Plop.

"So would I, really," said the little

girl. "I wanted a white mouse, but Mummy says that if a mouse comes into the house she will leave it, and I suppose Father Christmas didn't want me to be an orphan."

Plop was thinking. "I don't think owls have Father Christmas – not Barn Owls, anyway – and I haven't got a stocking to hang up."

"Aah, what a shame," said the little girl. "Everybody should have Father Christmas. It's so exciting waking up in the morning and feeling all the bumps in your stocking and trying to guess what is in it."

"Oh, stop it," wailed Plop. "I wish he would come to me."

"Shut your eyes," the little girl said. "Go on. Shut them and you may get a surprise."

Plop shut his eyes tight and waited.

The little girl quickly pulled off her wellington and took off a sock. She was wearing two pairs because the boots were a bit big for her.

"Open your eyes!" she said to Plop,

holding up the sock while she stood on one leg and wriggled her foot back into her wellington.

Plop opened his eyes – and then shut them again because he couldn't believe what he saw.

"Don't you want it?" said the little girl. "I know it's a bit holey, but I don't expect Father Christmas will mind."

"Oh, thank you," said Plop, taking it with his beak and then holding it in his foot. "Thank you *very* much. I'll go and hang it up at once."

"Not yet," laughed the little girl. "You'll have to wait until Christmas Eve. Well, I must go now. It must be nearly tea-time. Goodbye. I do hope Father Christmas will come to you."

"Goodbye," said Plop, bobbing his funny little bow. "You are very kind. You are a proper girl."

"And you have a very nice 'Eeek' !" said the little girl. "I'm going to practise it to make my brothers jump. EEEK!" She ran off, and Plop could hear her 'eeeking' right across the field.

Plop picked up the sock in his beak, and flew up to the landing branch.

"Well?" said his mother.

"Jah lijjle yirl shays – " he began with his mouth full of sock. He put it down and tried again. "The little girl says DARK IS NECESSARY, because of Father Christmas coming," he said.

"And what do you think, Plop?"

"I still do not like it AT ALL – but I'm going to hang up this sock on Christmas Eve."

And Plop took his sock and put it away very carefully in a corner of the nest-hole ready for Christmas.

DARK IS FASCINATING

Plop, having slept nearly all day, was very lively that evening – very lively and very hungry. He kept wobbling along the branch to where his father was roosting to see if by chance he were awake and ready to go hunting.

Mr Barn Owl was drawn up tall and still. He seemed hardly to be breathing. Plop stretched up on tiptoe and tried to see into his father's face. What a strong, curved beak he had.

"Daddy, are you awake?" he said loudly. "I'm hungry."

Mr Barn Owl did not open his eyes, but the beak moved.

"Go away!" it said. "I'm asleep."

Plop went away obediently – and then realised something and went back again. "Daddy! You can't be asleep. You spoke – I heard you."

"You must have imagined it," said his father, still not opening his eyes.

"You spoke," said Plop. "You're awake, so you can go hunting." He butted his father's tummy with his head. "Come on! It's getting-up time!"

Mr Barn Owl sighed and stretched. "All right, all right, you horrible owlet. What time is it?" He looked up at the sky. "Suffering bats! It isn't even dark yet! I could have had another half hour." He glared at Plop. "Dash it, I'm going to have another half hour. I will not be bullied by an addled little

– little DAY BIRD. Go away! You may wake me when it is dark, and not before, d'you understand?" He suddenly leaned forward until his huge beak was level with Plop's own little carpet tack. Plop could see two of himself reflected in his father's eyes.

"Er – yes, Daddy," he said, backing away hurriedly.

"Good," said his father, drawing himself up to sleep again. "Good day."

Plop went back to the nest-hole to complain to his mother. A sleepy Mrs Barn Owl listened sympathetically.

"Well, dear, I should go and find out some more about the world if I were you," she said. "Look! There's a young lady down there. Why don't you go and talk to her?"

Plop peered down through the leaves. Standing a little way from the tree

was someone wearing
shiny black boots, a
bright red fur coat
with a matching hat,
and what looked like
a white beard.

"That's not a young
lady!" shrieked Plop.
"That's Father Christmas!"
And he fell off his branch
in such a hurry that he forgot either to
shut his eyes *or* to take a deep breath.

He landed quite well, considering,
but lost his balance at the last moment
and toppled forward on to his face.

A gentle hand picked him up and set
him right way up again.

"Oh, you poor darling," said a sweet
young voice. "Are you all right?"

Plop looked up quickly. That voice
didn't sound right.

It wasn't a white beard – it was long blond hair.

"You're not Father Christmas at all!" he said crossly. "And I came down *specially*."

"I'm terribly sorry," said the young lady.

"And I'm not a darling. I'm a Barn Owl."

"I tell you what," the Father Christmas Lady said. "May I draw a picture of you in my Nature Sketch Book? I haven't got a Barn Owl in it."

"Me?" said Plop. "You mean *really* me?"

"Yes, please. Perhaps you could pose on that low branch for me."

Plop fluttered up to the branch and stood stiffly to attention. The Father Christmas Lady sat on a log and began to draw.

"I always carry my sketch book about with me in case I see something interesting," she said.

The interesting Barn Owl drew himself up proudly like a soldier in a sentry box.

But not for long. The young lady looked up from her drawing to find that her Barn Owl had completely disappeared.

"Can I see?" said a small voice down by her boot. Plop was jiggling up and down trying to see what was on the pad.

"There's not much to see, yet," she said, "but all right – you can look."

Plop looked. "I'm not bald like that!" he said indignantly.

"I haven't had time to get you properly

dressed," said the young lady.

"And you've only given me one leg."

"I'm afraid a bald, one-legged Barn Owl is all there's going to be unless you keep still."

Plop really tried very hard after that, and he only got down three or four times to see how she was getting on.

He could hardly believe his eyes when it was finished. "Is that really me?" he said. "I look just like Daddy – well, almost."

"Yes, that's really you," she said. "I keep one end of the book for animals and birds that come out in the day-time and the other end for night creatures. I've put you with them, of course."

"Oh," said Plop. "Er – of course."

"All the most interesting ones are your end," the young lady went on. "I think DARK IS FASCINATING."

"I – er – *tell* me about it," said Plop. (Well, it was too late now to tell her that she had got him at the wrong end of the book!)

"Hop up then," said the young lady, holding out a finger and taking Plop on to her lap, "and I'll show you what good company you are in. Look – here are some badgers."

Plop looked at the big black and white animals with stripes down their noses. "Funny faces they've got."

"That's so they don't bump into each other in the dark," explained the young lady. "They can't see very well."

She turned over the page. "Ah! Now I think these are the most fascinating night creatures of all – bats."

"You've got it the wrong way up," said Plop.

The Father Christmas lady laughed.

"No, I haven't. That's how bats like to be when they're not fluttering about – hanging upside down by their feet."

"Go on!" said Plop.

"Yes, really. And do you know, if you were a baby bat your mother would take you with her wherever she went, clinging to her fur. You'd get lots of rides."

"Oh, I'd like that," Plop said.

"Yes, but when you got too big to be carried, do you know what your mother would do? She'd hang you up before she went out!"

"Hang me up?" said Plop. "Upside down?"

"That's right. Now, let's see what else we can find." She turned a few pages. "Yes, here we are – oh!"

Plop was not with her.

He was rocking backwards and forwards on the low branch like one of those little wobbly men that you push. Every now and then he went a bit too far and had to waggle his wings to keep his balance.

"What are you doing?" asked the young lady.

"I'm trying to be a bat," said Plop, "but what I don't understand is how

63

they begin. I can't *get* upside down."

"Perhaps it would be easier to be a hedgehog," said the young lady. "When they're frightened they roll themselves into a ball, look – here's a picture of one."

Plop hopped back on to her knee and inspected the hedgehog.

"His feathers could do with a bit of fluffing up," he said.

"Those aren't feathers – they're prickles. Very useful they are, too. A hedgehog can jump off quite a high fence without hurting himself because he makes himself into a prickly ball and just bounces."

"Very useful," said Plop. "I wish I had prickles." He jumped off her lap and tried to roll himself into a ball.

It was very difficult. "I don't seem to have enough bends," he said.

Suddenly he stopped rolling about and stayed still, listening. Then he rushed back to the young lady's lap and tried to bury himself in her coat.

"What's the matter?" she said.

"THERE'S A FUNNY NOISE," he said. "OVER THERE."

The young lady listened. There was a busy, rustling sound coming from the dry leaves under the big tree.

"Why, I do believe it's a hedgehog!"

she said. "Yes, here he is. Look!"

Plop peeped cautiously over the edge of her lap. A tiny pointed snout pushed its way through the leaves, and then a small round creature scuttled across the ground in front of them.

"They never bother to move about quietly," the young lady whispered, "because they know nobody would want to eat anything so prickly."

"Is he sure?" said Plop. "I'm so hungry I could eat anything!"

The hedgehog stopped dead and rolled himself into a tight little ball.

"He must have heard you," the young lady said reproachfully. "What a thing to say."

"Well, it's true," Plop said. "I'm starving."

"Oh, of course! You'll be going hunting with your parents now that it's getting dark, won't you? I was forgetting you're a night bird."

The night bird looked down at his toes.

"Well, I won't keep you," she went on, "except – would you mind doing something for me before you go? I *would* like to hear you screech."

Plop didn't mind at all. He stuck out his chest and gave her the most enormous "EEEEEEEK!" he could possibly manage.

"Gorgeous!" said the young lady.

Plop bobbed his funny little bow. Then he took off and circled round, 'eeking' for all he was worth. The young lady waved, and then with one final 'eeeek!' of farewell, Plop flew up to the landing branch.

"Well?" said his mother.

"The Father Christmas Lady – you

were right, it was a lady – says DARK IS FASCINATING."

"And what do you think, Plop?"

"I still do not like it AT ALL. But what do you think? The lady drew a picture of me."

"Well, that's very special, isn't it? Nobody has ever put me in a picture."

"*And* she says my screech is gorgeous."

"She does, does she? I wondered what all that noise was about."

"Where's Daddy?"

"Out hunting."

"Oh, jolly good. I could eat a hedge-hog!"

"I wouldn't recommend it," said his mother.

DARK IS WONDERFUL

"That was nice," said Plop when he had gulped down what his father had brought. "What was it?"

"A shrew," said his father.

"I like shrew," said Plop. "What's next?"

"A short pause," said Mrs Barn Owl. "Let your poor Daddy get his breath back."

"All right," said Plop, "but do hurry up, Daddy. Shrews are nice, but they're not very big, are they? This one feels very lonely all by itself at the bottom of my tummy. It needs company."

"I don't believe there is a bottom to your tummy," said his father. "No matter how much I put into it, it is never full. Oh well, I suppose I had better go and hunt for something else to cast into the bottomless pit."

"That's what fathers are for," said Plop. "Wouldn't you like to go hunting, too, Mummy? It would be a nice change for you."

"Thank you very much," said Mrs Barn Owl. "What you really mean is that you won't have to wait so long between courses! But I will certainly go if you don't mind being left."

"Why don't you come with us?" said his father. "Then you wouldn't have to wait at all."

Plop looked round at the creeping darkness. "Er – no, thank you, Daddy," he said. "I have some more remembering to do."

"Right'o," said Mr Barn Owl. "Ready, dear?"

Plop's parents took off together side by side, their great white wings almost touching. Plop sat outside the nesthole and watched them drift away into

the darkness until they melted into each other and then disappeared altogether. It took quite a long time, because the stars were coming out and Plop could see a long way by their light with his owl's eyes.

He remembered what his mother had said about dark never being black. It certainly was not black tonight. It was more of a misty grey, and the sky was pricked all over with tiny stars.

"Drat!" said a voice from somewhere below Plop.

Plop started and peered down through the leaves. There was a man with some sort of contraption set up in front of him, standing there scowling up at the cloud which had hidden the moon. What was he doing?

Plop shut his eyes, took a deep breath, and fell off his branch.

He shot through the air like a white
streak and landed with a soft bump.

"Heavens!" cried the man. "A shooting star!"

"Actually, I'm a Barn Owl," said the

shooting star. "What's that thing you've got there?"

"A telescope," said the man. "A Barn Owl, did you say? Well, well. I thought you were a meteor. How do you do?"

"How do I do what?" asked Plop.

"Oh – you know what I mean. How are you?"

"Hungry," said Plop. "I thought you said I was a shooting star, not a meteor."

"A meteor *is* a shooting star."

"Oh," said Plop. "What is the television for?"

"Telescope. For looking at things like the stars and planets."

"Ooh! Can I have a look, please?"

"Of course," said the man, "but it's not a very good night for it, I'm afraid. Too cloudy."

"I don't like the dark very much," said Plop.

"Really?" said the man. "How very odd. You must miss such a lot. DARK IS WONDERFUL."

"Tell me," said Plop. "Please."

"I'll do better than that – I'll show you," the man said. "Come and put your eye – no, no! *This* end!"

Plop had jumped up, scuttled along the telescope, and was now peering backwards between his feet into the wrong end.

"I can't see anything," he said.

"You surprise me," said the man. "Try this end."

Plop wobbled back along the telescope and the man supported him on his wrist so that his eye was level with the eye-piece.

"Now can you see anything?"

75

"Oh yes," said Plop. "It makes everything come nearer, doesn't it? I can see a bright, bright star. That must be very near."

"Yes – just fifty four million, million miles away, that's all."

"Million, million – !" gasped Plop.

"Yes, that's Sirius, the Dog Star. You're quite right – it is one of the nearest." Obviously million millions were nothing to the man with a telescope.

"Why is it called the Dog Star?" asked Plop.

"Because it belongs to Orion, the Great Hunter. Look! There he is. Can you see those three stars close together?"

76

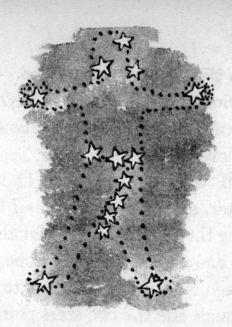

Plop drew his head back from the telescope and blinked.

"Can I change eyes?" he said. "This one's getting very tired."

"Yes, of course. Now – see if you can find the Great Hunter."

"He has three stars close together, did you say?"

"Yes – that's his belt."

"And some fainter stars behind him?"

"Yes – that's his sword."

"I've got him!" shouted Plop. "I've got Orion the Great Hunter. Oh, I never knew stars had names. Show me some more."

"Well, we'll see if we can find the Pole Star, shall we? Hang on – I have to swing the telescope round for that."

Plop had a ride on the telescope, and then the man showed him how to find the Plough and the two stars pointing straight up to the Pole Star. "That's a bright one, too, isn't it?" said Plop.

"Yes. There! Now you can find that, you need never get lost, because that star is directly over the North Pole so you'll always know where north is."

"Is that important?" asked Plop.

"Very important," said the man. "Heavens! What was that?" An eerie, long-drawn shriek had torn the peace of the night.

78

"Oh dear. I expect that's my Daddy," said Plop. They looked up. A ghostly, whitish form circled above them. "Yes, it is. I'd better let him know I'm here. Eeeeeek!"

"Oh!" said the man, jumping. "You should warn people when you're going to do that. You know, I've often wondered what that noise was. Now I shall know it is only you or your father."

"Or my mother," said Plop. "I really must go. Thank you very, very much for teaching me about the stars." He hopped on to the telescope and bowed his funny little bow. "Goodbye."

"Goodbye, Master Barn Owl. Good star-gazing!"

Plop flew up to join his father and together they landed on the landing branch.

"Well?" said Plop's mother.

"The man with the telescope says DARK IS WONDERFUL, and he called me 'Master Barn Owl' and . . ."

"And what do you think, Plop?"

"I know what *I* think," said Mr Barn Owl, not giving Plop a chance to reply. "I think Master Barn Owl has got a bit of a cheek to send his poor parents on an absolutely urgent search for food and then not bother to be in when they get back. I thought you were supposed to be starving?"

"I *am* starving," said Plop, "but did you know that the Dog Star is fifty-four million, million miles away . . ."

"Do you want your dinner or don't you?" said Mr Barn Owl.

"Oh yes," said Plop. He gobbled down what his father had brought, and he gobbled down what his mother had brought, and not only did he not ask what it was that he had just eaten, but he did not even say "What's next?"

What he said was, "Daddy, do you know how to find the Pole Star? Shall I show you?"

"By all means," said Mr Barn Owl, giving his wife a slow wink. "Anything that can take your mind off your tummy like this *must* be worth seeing!"

Plop would not rest – and so neither could Mr and Mrs Barn Owl – until he had made quite sure that they could recognise all the stars which the man with the telescope had shown him.

He was still at it at about four o'clock in the morning.

"Now are you quite sure you understand about the Pole Star?" he said to his mother, who seemed to be being a bit dense about it.

"I think so, dear," yawned Mrs Barn Owl. "You find the thing that looks like a plough but is actually a big bear – or is it a small bear? – and the Pole Star is – um – near the North Star."

"The Pole Star *is* the North Star," Plop said impatiently, "and the two stars at the front of the Plough point to it. I don't think you're really trying. You haven't been listening."

"Oh, we have," said Mr Barn Owl. "We have been listening for hours and hours. I think perhaps Mummy is just a little bit tired . . ."

"But you must know how to find the Pole Star," said Plop, "or you might get lost."

"I never get lost," said his father indignantly, "and neither does your mother. Now be a good chap and go into the nest-hole and I'll see if I can find you something nice for your supper. You can have it in bed for once, hmm?"

"Oh, all right," said Plop, "but I really do feel that you should know about these things. I'll have to try to explain again tomorrow."

Mr Barn Owl turned to his wife in horror. "Oh, no! Not tomorrow night as well! I couldn't stand it."

"Never mind, dear," said Mrs Barn Owl soothingly. "You haven't had to do nearly as much hunting as usual."

"I'm not at all sure that all this star-gazing isn't much more wearing than filling the bottomless pit!" groaned Mr Barn Owl.

"Oh, Daddy." Plop put his head out of the nest-hole. "Did I tell you about Orion? Orion is the Great Hunter and – oh, he's gone!"

"Yes, dear, he must finish his hunting before it gets light," said his mother. "Now you get back in there and mind you wash behind your ears properly. I'm coming to inspect you in a minute."

So Plop had his supper in bed. And then, like a real night owl, he slept right through the daylight hours.

DARK IS BEAUTIFUL

When Plop woke up, it was already getting dark. He came out on to the landing branch. There was an exciting frosty nip in the air. "Now who's a day bird!" Plop shouted at the darkness. "I am what I am!"

"What *is* he bellowing about?" said Mr Barn Owl, waking up with a start.

"I believe Plop is beginning to enjoy being an owl at last," said Mrs Barn Owl, "but ssh! Pretend to be asleep."

Plop waddled up to inspect them. They were drawn up tall. Fancy sleeping on such a lovely night! Well, he wasn't going to hang about waiting for them. He might be missing something. The man with a telescope might be back, or some Boy Scouts, or anything. He was going down to see.

So Plop shut his eyes, took a deep breath, and fell off his branch.

He floated down on his little white wings and landed like a feather. Feeling very pleased with himself, he looked around.

There were two strange lamps shining from the shadows under the tree. Plop went closer, and found that the lamps were a pair of unwinking eyes, and they belonged to a big black cat. Plop waited for a minute, but what he was expecting to happen didn't.

"Aren't you going to say anything?" he said at last. "All the others did."

"What should I say?" drawled the cat.

"Well, what did you think I was?" said Plop. "I've been mistaken for a Catherine-wheel, and a thunderbolt, and a woolly ball, and a darling and a shooting star, and even a roly-poly pudding. Don't I remind you of anything?"

"You look like a baby owl to me," said the cat. Then, seeing Plop's disappointed face, he added, "but I *did* wonder for a moment whether it was starting to snow."

"You thought I was a snowflake?" said Plop, brightening.

"Yes, but then when you landed, I saw that you looked more like a fat little snowman," said the cat, "and then I knew you were a baby owl."

"Ah, but do you know what *kind* of owl I am?" said Plop.

"No," admitted the cat, "I can't say I do."

"I am a Barn Owl," Plop said.

"Really?" said the cat. "Well, I'm a House Cat, I suppose. My name is Orion."

"Orion! The Great Hunter!" breathed Plop.

"Well, thank you," said the cat, stroking his fine whiskers with a modest paw. "I am rather a good mouser, as a matter of fact, but I didn't know I was as famous as that."

"Orion," said Plop again. "Oh, I wish I had a name like that."

"What is your name?" asked the cat.

"Plop," said Plop. "Isn't it awful?"

"Oh, I don't know – it's – er – different," the cat said kindly, "and at least it's short. There's nothing short for Orion really, so I'm usually called

'Puss', which I can't say I care for."

"I shall call you Orion," said Plop.

"Thank you. Look – er – Plop. I was just going hunting. Would you like to come with me?"

"Oh," said Plop. "I don't know. I would like to, I think, but I'm not very happy about the dark."

"Oh dear. We'll have to do something about that," said Orion.

"What?" said Plop. "What can you do when you're afraid of the dark?"

"I don't believe you are afraid of the dark, really," said Orion. "You just think you are. DARK IS BEAUTIFUL. Take a night like this. Look around you. Isn't it beautiful?"

Plop looked. The moon had risen. Everything was bathed in its white light.

"I love moonlight," said the cat.

"Moonlight is magic. It turns everything it touches to silver, especially on
frosty nights like this. Oh, come with
me, Plop, and I will show you a beautiful world of sparkling silver – the
secret night-time world of cats and
owls. The daytime people are asleep. It
is all ours, Plop. Will you come?"

"Yes!" said Plop. "I will. Just wait
while I tell Mummy where I'm going,"
He flew like an arrow up to the landing
branch.

"Well?" said his mother.

"Orion says that DARK IS BEAUTI-
FUL, and he has asked me to go hunt-
ing with him. I can go, can't I,
Mummy?"

"Of course, dear. But who is Orion?"

"The Great Hunter!" said Plop. "See
you later."

When Mr Barn Owl came in from his

first expedition, he found his wife a bit agitated.

"I think all that star-gazing has gone to Plop's head," she said. "He said he was going hunting with Orion the Great Hunter. That was one of the stars he showed us last night, wasn't it?"

"Well, I saw him just now with a perfectly ordinary black cat," said Mr Barn Owl. "They were pussy-footing it up among the chimney pots on those houses near the church."

"So far from home – are you *sure* it was Plop you saw?" said Mrs Barn Owl.

It was indeed Plop he had seen. Orion had taken him up to his roof-top world, the cat leading the way, climbing and leaping, Plop fluttering behind.

They sat together on the highest roof and looked down over the sleeping town, a black velvet cat and a little white powder puff of owl.

"Well?" said the cat.

"It is – it is – oh, I haven't the words for it," breathed Plop. "But you are right, Orion. I am a night bird after all. Fancy sleeping all night and missing this!"

"And this is only one sort of night,"

said Orion. "There are lots of other kinds, all beautiful. There are hot, scented summer nights; and cold windy nights when the scuffling clouds make ragged shadows across the ground; and breathless, thundery nights which are suddenly slashed with jagged white lightning; and fresh spring nights, when even the day-birds

can't bear to sleep; and muffled winter nights when snow blankets the ground and ices the houses and trees. Oh, the nights I have seen – and you will see, Plop, as a night bird."

"Yes," said Plop. "This is my world, Orion. I must go home."

"What, already? We haven't done any hunting yet, and I have lots more to show you – a glass lake with the moon floating in it, and . . ."

"I must go, Orion. I want to surprise them. Thank you for – for showing me that I'm a night bird."

He bobbed his funny little bow and the black cat solemnly bowed back. "Goodbye, Plop," he said, "and many, many Good Nights!"

Plop took off, circled once, gave a final "Eek!" of farewell, and then flew, straight and sure, back to his tree.

"Well?" said his mother.

Plop took a deep breath. "The small boy said DARK IS EXCITING. The old lady said DARK IS KIND. The Boy Scout said DARK IS FUN. The little girl said DARK IS NECESSARY. The Father Christmas Lady said DARK IS FASCINATING. The man with the telescope said DARK IS WONDERFUL and Orion the black cat says DARK IS BEAUTIFUL."

"And what do you think, Plop?"

Plop looked up at his mother with twinkling eyes. "I think," he said. "I think – DARK IS SUPER! But Sssh! Daddy's coming. Don't say anything."

Mr Barn Owl came in with a great flapping of wings. He dropped something at Plop's feet.

Plop swallowed it in one gulp. "That was nice," he said. "What was it?"

"A vole."

"I like vole," said Plop. "What's next?"

"Why don't you come with me and find out?" said Mr Barn Owl.

"Yes, please," said Plop.

Mr Barn Owl blinked. "What did you say?"

"I said 'yes, please'," Plop said. "I would like to come hunting with you."

"I thought you were afraid of the dark!"

"Me?" said Plop. "Afraid of the dark! That was a *long* time ago!"

"Well!" said his father. "What are we waiting for? A-hunting we will go!"

"Hey, wait for me," said Plop's mother. "I'm coming too."

So they took off together in the moonlight, Mr and Mrs Barn Owl on each side and Plop in the middle.

Plop – the night bird.

The Cat Who
Wanted to Go Home

1 An unusual basket

Suzy was a little striped cat. She had stiffly starched white whiskers and a fine pair of football socks on her front paws.

Suzy lived in the house of a fisherman in a little seaside village in France. The fisherman had four sons. Pierre was ten years old, Henri was eight, Paul was six and Gaby was four, so when they stood in a row they looked like a set of steps. All the boys played with Suzy and they took her with them everywhere.

Pierre, the eldest one, made Suzy a

scratching-post by wrapping a bit of old carpet round one of the fat legs of the big kitchen table. Suzy could sharpen her claws whenever she liked.

Henri knew which were the best tickly places on her spotted tummy. Although all the rest of her was covered with black stripes, Suzy's tummy was fawn with black spots. Henri said she was a tiger on top and a leopard underneath. Anyway, he was a jolly good tickler.

Paul made a toy for her. He tied a piece of crackly paper to the end of a long piece of string and pulled it along on the ground for her to chase. Suzy could run very fast and Paul could not keep ahead of her for very long. She would pounce and catch the paper again and again. Paul would stand still to get his breath back and dangle the bit of paper just out of reach above her head. Suzy would leap and leap to catch it, with Paul jerking it away when she got too near. Paul was great fun.

But Gaby, the youngest, was the best. Suzy adored him – and for a very odd reason. Gaby didn't know the proper way to stroke a cat. Most cats like being stroked from head to tail, the way the fur lies. But Gaby always stroked Suzy the wrong way – backwards from tail to head – and Suzy *loved* it. She would wriggle against his hand with delight, purring like a sewing machine, asking him to do it again and again. She liked it better than anything in the world. Yes, even better than eating fish. And Suzy liked eating fish very much indeed – which was just as well because she had it for breakfast and supper every day.

The boys always helped their father when he came home in his boat with his catch of fish. Every day they waited for him on the quay – Pierre and Henri and Paul and Gaby and Suzy. She was allowed to eat as much as she wanted of the fish that were too small to be sold. There was always something for Suzy even when the catch wasn't very good. She would have grown fat if the boys had not given her so much exercise.

Suzy hated it when the boys were at school and there was nobody to play with her; nobody to dangle a bit of string or throw a ball or to climb trees with her. She would wander round the quay by herself getting in every-body's way, or go exploring in the fields behind the village.

One day she was chasing butterflies across a field when she nearly bumped into a huge basket. Suzy was used to baskets – there were lots of them on the quay – but this one was much bigger. Suzy climbed up the steep side and peered in. The basket was so big that there was a wooden stool inside. Under the stool was a nice patch of shade.

It was a very hot day. Suzy decided to have a little nap. She jumped lightly down into the basket and settled herself nose to tail under the stool. Curled round like that she looked like a huge furry snail.

Suzy was soon fast asleep.

When she woke up Suzy felt very peculiar.

The basket seemed to be rocking from side to side, joggling her. She rushed to the edge of the basket and climbed up the side to jump out – but she changed her mind when she looked over the top! The ground was a very long way away – much too far for her to jump. She clung on tightly as the basket jerked again, grabbing at a rope with her paws.

Ropes? She had not noticed them when she climbed in. Suzy looked up. The ropes were attached to a huge balloon – an *enormous* balloon. Suzy was floating high up in the sky in a basket suspended from a balloon!

Poor Suzy! She slid back into the basket and crouched on the floor, shivering with fright.

Then she felt a gentle hand on her back and looked up to find that there was a man in the basket with her.

'Hello, little cat,' he said. 'I didn't invite you! Oh well, it's too late now. You will have to come with me to England.'

Suzy didn't know where England was, but she knew she didn't want to go there. She wanted to stay in France in her own little fishing village with the boys.

'Chez-moi!' she wailed. It sounded like 'shay-mwa'. She was saying in French that she wanted to go home.

But the man had to jump up to do something with the balloon, which was swinging wildly, and from then on was too busy to take any notice of his little passenger.

So Suzy floated across the sea between France and England by balloon! She hated every joggly moment of it. The worst part was seeing the coast of France disappear behind them – France and Pierre and Henri and Paul and Gaby, France and everything she knew and loved.

'Chez-moi!' she wailed again, but nobody heard her. There were big puffy clouds sailing underneath them and sometimes what looked like toy ships on the sea far below. It was really very interesting and beautiful, but Suzy could only think about one thing. How was she going to get back across this huge stretch of water?

They landed in England with a bump. Suzy had not realized that they were back over land again because for the last bit she had had her eyes tightly shut. She jumped out of the basket and ran. She could not get away from that balloon fast enough.

Because she was very hungry, she ran towards a fishy smell. But the smell was coming from the sea and there were no fish and no fishing boats. This was an English seaside town and not a bit like her own village. There was just a wide expanse of concrete in front of the sea, with steps down to the sand. Poor Suzy. She sat miserably on the sea-front looking out at the waves. How was she going to get home across all that water?

Luckily an RSPCA lady came along. It was her job to find homes for lost cats. She

picked up
Suzy and
took her to
the house of
a kind old
lady whom she
knew, called Auntie Jo.
'Do you think you could
look after this little cat for me,
Auntie Jo?' the RSPCA lady said. 'I've never
seen her before. She's not from around here.
She must be lost.'

'Of course she can stay with me,' said
Auntie Jo. 'She'll be company for Biff.'

Biff was Auntie Jo's new budgie who was
just learning to talk.

'Hello, Auntie Jo,' he said in his funny
cracked voice.

Of course, Suzy could not understand

English, but she understood the saucer of milk that Auntie Jo put down for her and she lapped up every drop. Then, because she was a polite cat, she said 'thank you' in French: 'Merci!' It was a miaowing sound, 'mare-see'.

'What a funny miaow you have, Pussy cat,' said Auntie Jo.

'Merci,' said Biff.

'Oh, clever Biff,' Auntie Jo said.

'Clever Biff,' said Biff. 'Merci.'

Suzy was made very comfortable on an old chair that night. Auntie Jo stroked her gently and Suzy purred. She purred in French, but purring sounds the same all over the world, whatever country you come from.

But it wasn't like home. She did miss Gaby stroking her the wrong way.

2   *Up and down is no good*

So Suzy came to live with Auntie Jo and Biff.

Next morning Auntie Jo got out her tricycle to go shopping. It was a great big one with huge wheels and a basket on the front. Auntie Jo felt that she was too old to wobble about on a bicycle any more, and what was good enough for the little girl next door was good enough for her.

When Suzy saw Auntie Jo standing in front of the mirror in the hall, fiercely jabbing a hat pin into her flat straw hat to keep it anchored to her bun, she guessed that Auntie Jo was going out.

When Auntie Jo had pedalled a few yards down the road she suddenly saw a whiskery face staring at her over the handlebars.

'Chez-moi!' it said.

Auntie Jo swerved violently and stopped.

'Oh, Pussy! You did frighten me. What are you doing in there? Go home. Shoo!'

Suzy didn't understand.

'Chez-moi!' she wailed again, settling herself more comfortably in the basket.

'Oh, very well, you can come if you want to,' said Auntie Jo, starting to pedal again. 'But sit still.'

So Suzy rode down to the sea-front in great style in Auntie Jo's tricycle basket. She got very excited when she saw the sea. That sheet of blue water with white lace trimmings was all that lay between her and France. Oh, she would soon be home.

The minute Auntie Jo had parked the tricycle by the butcher's shop and disappeared inside, Suzy jumped down from the basket and ran across the road to the beach. There were children everywhere, digging in the sand and running about with buckets of water, just like French children. Suzy dodged nimbly between them and ran down to the water's edge. She had hoped to find a fishing boat like the one belonging to her family, but there didn't seem to be anything like that – only lots of people shouting and splashing in the water. She was so busy staring out to sea, looking for boats, that she hardly noticed the wavelets trickling across the sand and washing over her paws.

'Oh, look! There's a kitten over there,

paddling!' a little girl said to her father, who was sitting in a deckchair reading his paper.

'Kittens don't paddle, Caroline,' he said. 'Cats hate water.'

'Well, this one is paddling,' said Caroline. 'I'm going down to watch her.'

She dropped her spade and ran down to the sea. Suzy had moved along a bit, but she was easy to find because of the trail of paw-prints she left behind her in the sand.

'Pussy!' said Caroline, putting down her hand and stroking Suzy. Suzy trilled and purred and rubbed against the little girl's hand.

'Oh, you are sweet,' she said, picking her up and holding her against her shoulder. 'Come on, I want to show you to Daddy. He doesn't believe that you've been paddling.'

She started back up the beach, but Suzy

suddenly jumped down and tore away across the sand towards some rocks. She had seen something! From Caroline's shoulder she had had a better view over the top of people's heads, and she was sure she had seen a boat. A boat! She could get home at last.

Caroline started to follow her, but Suzy was going much too fast, and anyway her father would be cross if she just disappeared without telling him where she was going. Bother! Now he would never believe that there *had* been a paddling kitten.

Suzy reached the rocks, and looked about her. Yes! There was the boat. It was a very small plastic canoe, but it was all there was so it would have to do. A small boy was paddling it along close to the rocks. Suzy scrambled towards him over the slippery seaweed and fixed him with her great green eyes.

'Chez-moi!' she called hopefully. 'Chez-moi!'

The boy looked up and stared at her in amazement. He had never seen a cat on the beach before.

'What do you want, Puss? Not a ride, surely?'

Suzy answered by taking a firm grip on the seaweed and leaping neatly into the canoe. She curled her tail round her toes and waited patiently. She was on her way home at last.

But of course she was not. People don't cross the Channel in toy canoes. The little boy was only allowed to go up and down in the shallow water close to the shore. After a few minutes of going up and down, up and down, Suzy began to get restless. This was no good. This wouldn't get her home to France.

'Chez-moi!' she wailed. Why didn't the boy understand how important it was to her to get home? 'Chez-moi!'

'Oh, you want to get out now, do you?' he said. 'Right'o, hang on a tick.'

He pulled in towards a flat rock. When Suzy realized that he was taking her back to land she gave up all hope of getting to France on this trip. She got ready to spring.

'Mind your claws!' shouted the little boy suddenly, as he saw her digging them into the plastic canoe. 'You'll puncture us!'

It was too late, and Suzy didn't understand anyway. She sprang out on to the rock, leaving behind four sets of tiny holes from which the air hissed fiercely. Claws are not good for inflated plastic.

The boy sprang out too, pulling the canoe after him.

'That's the last time I give a ride to a cat,' he grumbled, fishing in his pocket for his repair kit.

The canoe slowly collasped and was quite flat by the time Suzy was back by the butcher's shop. Auntie Jo's tricycle wasn't there, but Suzy remembered the way to her house.

'Pussy cat, Pussy cat, where have you been?' said Auntie Jo when Suzy walked in.

'Pussy cat, Pussy cat, where have you been?' Biff repeated in his funny voice. 'Clever Biff.'

'You are a clever Biff,' said Auntie Jo. 'Well, Pussy cat, here is your dinner.' She put down a saucer of liver.

Suzy ate it all up. It wasn't fish, but it was very nice.

'Merci,' she said, cleaning her whiskers.

'You do have a funny miaow,' said Auntie Jo.

'Merci,' Biff said. 'Clever Biff.'

And Suzy purred.

But she did miss Gaby stroking her the wrong way.

3   *They do it for fun*

Next morning Auntie Jo got out her tricycle again. Suzy hopped into the basket. It was very windy and Auntie Jo had to hang on to her hat all the way down to the shops.

As they came round the corner on to the sea-front they were nearly knocked over. The wind was blowing fiercely from the sea. There were huge waves thundering on the beach.

Auntie Jo managed to park by the grocer's. Suzy went to look at the waves. There would be no chance of getting home to France that day.

Or was there? A young man was pushing his way into the waves holding a flat board above his head. He was definitely going out to sea *towards France*!

Suzy ran towards him, but she was too late; he was already a long way out. He was swimming now, pushing the board in front of him.

She watched him sadly. He was going without her. She had so wanted to go home. Suzy threw back her head and wailed:

'Chez-moi!'

But what was this? The young man must have heard her, because he was coming back. He was coming back for her!

Suzy ran to meet him, not caring how wet she got. He jumped off the board as it grounded on the sand, and Suzy jumped on to it. The young man *was* surprised.

'Do you want to come surfing with me?' he asked. 'I thought cats didn't like water!'

'Chez-moi!' Suzy said.

'Okay. Hang on, though. It's kind of wet out there.'

The young man lifted the surf-board with Suzy on it high above his head, and set off through the waves.

Suzy had to work hard at keeping her balance, but she was happy. France at last.

She was not quite so happy when the young man began swimming, pushing the board in front of him, sometimes *through* the waves. But Suzy just closed her eyes and hung on, spitting out the nasty sea water when she got a mouthful.

Suddenly the young man shouted, 'Here comes a beauty!'

He swung the board round, kneeled on it,

and then stood up. A huge wave picked them up and hurtled them back toward the beach – to England. Suzy was furious.

'Chez-moi!' she wailed.

'Yes, isn't it marvellous!' shouted the young man. He thought she was enjoying it as much as he was.

There were some more young men with boards on the beach. They were very surprised to see Suzy.

'Whatever have you got there, Bill?' shouted one of them. 'A new member for the club?'

'Yes,' Bill shouted. 'She's terrific. A real swinger. You watch.'

They all set off out to sea. Suzy was very relieved. Of course, he had just come back for the others, that was all. Now they would go to France.

But, of course, they didn't. They went out

to sea and back again several times before Suzy realized that they were only doing it for fun!

The surf-riders thought Suzy was wonderful, and when they came out of the sea for lunch they made a great fuss of her. They rolled her in a towel to dry her off a bit and then fed her with a whole tin of sardines. Fish! Then they played ball with her and pulled a belt along the sand for her to chase.

Suzy had a lovely time – even if she didn't get home to France.

When she walked into Auntie Jo's house, Biff said:

'Pussy cat, Pussy cat, where have you been?'

'Yes, where have you been?' said Auntie Jo. 'Swimming, by the look of you. There's seaweed on your tail.'

Suzy sat down and washed herself all over. Auntie Jo pulled off the seaweed. Then she put down a saucer of mince.

Suzy ate it all up. It wasn't fish, but it was very good.

'Merci,' she said, cleaning her whiskers.

'You do have a funny miaow,' Auntie Jo said.

And Suzy purred.

But she did miss Gaby stroking her the wrong way.

4 Catty paddle

The next morning Auntie Jo got out her tricycle and Suzy hopped into the basket.

'I'm not sure that I should take you with me,' said Auntie Jo. 'You came back in such a horrible mess yesterday.'

'Chez-moi!' Suzy said, wondering why Auntie Jo didn't start.

'Oh, all right,' said Auntie Jo, 'but you behave yourself today.'

She pedalled off towards the shops. The wind had dropped, and when they came round the corner to the sea-front the sea was flat and calm like glass. Suzy was out of the basket before Auntie Jo had finished parking.

'Oh dear, she's off again,' said Auntie Jo, watching Suzy run down towards the sea. 'She is a funny little cat.'

The funny little cat was looking for *boats*. There must be some boats going to France on a nice calm day like this.

There were some pedal boats going up and down, but Suzy was getting wise. She knew that up and down was no good to her. She needed a boat that was going out to sea.

And there was one – a very fast speedboat. It was pulling a young girl along behind it! She was riding on the water on two long thin boards. She was going very fast. A boat like that would get you to France in no time.

Suzy ran down to the end of the pier. There was another speedboat getting ready to go, and there was another girl getting ready to be pulled behind.

Suzy watched her. She had hoped that one of the boats would pull *her* behind it, but those long water skis were much too big for her.

Then the girl got hold of a piece of rope that was dangling from the back of the speed-boat. Suzy wouldn't be able to hang on to that either, not with her tiny paws.

There was only one thing for it – she would have to go along with the girl.

Suzy jumped. She landed on the girl's shoulder, very gently, but the girl was not at all pleased.

'Get off!' she cried. 'What on earth . . . ?' She looked down sideways at her shoulder to see what this furry thing was, but she dare not let go of the rope to push it off because they would be starting any second.

'Oh get off!' she said again, trying to shove Suzy with her chin, but Suzy was not going to be pushed off that easily.

Then it was too late. With a great roar, the speedboat burst away from the pier. The girl tightened her grip on the rope and struggled to keep her balance on the skis, with Suzy teetering on her shoulder.

There were lots of people on the pier watching the water skiers, and they all laughed when they saw Suzy.

'A water-skiing cat!' they said. 'Just look at that!'

The water-skiing cat was having great difficulty in staying on. What could she hang on to? The girl had long hair. Suzy managed to get one paw tangled up in it and hung on to that.

'Ow!' cried the poor girl, but there was nothing she could do about it.

Suzy began to enjoy herself. It was very exciting going so fast, and she wasn't really getting wet at all except for a little spray. Oh, this was a lovely way to go home to France.

Then she noticed something. The other boat had turned round and was going back to the pier! Were they going to do the same?

Yes, their speedboat began to swerve. Suzy was so disappointed.

'Chez-moi!' she wailed loudly into the girl's ear.

It was too much for her. She jumped, lost her balance, and a second later she and Suzy were struggling in the water, the speedboat heading back for the pier without them.

Suzy headed for the pier too. She discovered that she could swim! She did a catty sort of dog-paddle.

Meanwhile, the crew in the boat realized that they had lost the water-skier and came back to pick her up.

'What happened to you?' asked the driver as he helped her into the boat.

'It was that wretched cat!' she said. 'It was all its fault.'

'What cat?' said the man. 'I can't see any cat.'

'Oh dear, she must have drowned, the poor little thing!' The water-skier was suddenly contrite. 'I was so busy trying to keep afloat myself I didn't notice what happened to her.'

'I did,' said the other man in the boat. 'She's swimming. Look! She's nearly at the pier already.'

There was Suzy, sodden and dripping, climbing on to the pier. All the people were cheering. The water-skier was so relieved that Suzy wasn't drowned that she forgave her at once.

Suzy dodged all the people and ran home to Auntie Jo.

'Pussy cat, Pussy cat, where have you been?' said Biff.

'You might well ask!' Auntie Jo said. She looked in horror at the soggy Suzy, dripping on her carpet. 'She's in an even worse state than she was yesterday.'

She rubbed Suzy all over hard with a rough towel and put on an electric fire for her to sit by until she was really dry.

Then she gave Suzy her dinner – a saucer of rabbit.

'I'm not sure you deserve it, though,' Auntie Jo said.

Suzy ate it all up. It wasn't fish, but it was very good.

'Merci,' she said, cleaning her whiskers.

Then Auntie Jo gave her a saucer of milk. It was lovely after all that salty water.

'Merci,' she said again.

'You do have a funny miaow,' Auntie Jo said. 'But you're a funny cat altogether.' She stroked her and Suzy purred.

But she did miss Gaby stroking her the wrong way.

5   *The wettest way*

The next morning Auntie Jo opened her newspaper – and there was a photograph of Suzy water-skiing!

'Well! So that's what you were up to yesterday, Pussy cat!' she said. 'No wonder you were so wet. I think you had better stay at home today.'

But when Auntie Jo wheeled out her tricycle, Suzy popped into the basket as usual.

'Chez-moi!' she said to Auntie Jo, beseeching her with her big green eyes.

'Oh, come on then,' Auntie Jo said.

134

As they pedalled along the sea-front to the shops, a lady and her husband recognized Suzy.

'Why surely that's the little cat who was water-skiing yesterday,' they said. 'So she belongs to you, does she, Auntie Jo?'

'She's a stray,' Auntie Jo said. 'I'm just feeding her.'

'Well, she's a very good swimmer,' said the lady.

'Yes,' said her husband. 'Let's hope she doesn't get any ideas because of what's happening today.'

'What is happening?' asked Auntie Jo.

'There's a swimmer attempting to cross the Channel. That's a very long way for a small cat.'

'Did you hear that, Pussy cat?' said Auntie Jo. 'No Channel swimming.'

But I'm afraid Suzy didn't understand, and when Auntie Jo parked her tricycle, she popped out of the basket as usual and ran down to the water's edge.

She was looking for boats, of course. There was one small boat and beside it was a great big fat man. It was the Channel swimmer. Somebody was smearing him all over with greasy stuff to keep him warm during his long swim.

Suzy wasn't very interested in all this until she heard somebody say, 'Well, good luck, Jim! Let's hope you get to France.'

France? He was really going to France!

So it was hardly surprising that when the man had been swimming for a few minutes he found that there was a little cat swimming beside him!

The man was swimming very slowly and

steadily because he had a long way to go, but even so it was a bit fast for Suzy, who was having to paddle madly to keep up with him. Clearly she wouldn't be able to do this for very long.

'Go home!' grunted the man.

Suzy didn't understand him, and anyway going home was what she was doing!

'What did you say, Jim?' said his wife, who was going along in the boat to see that he was all right.

'Company,' said Jim. 'Look!'

His wife thought he meant sharks or something.

'Good heavens!' she said. 'Where?'

'Cat,' said Jim.

'Cat?' Jim's wife peered through the waves. Then she saw Suzy.

Suzy was holding her head as high as she

could with her ears folded down to keep out the water. Jim's wife did laugh.

'You look like a mother duck and its baby, Jim,' she said. 'Shall I pick her up?'

'Leave her,' said Jim. 'She's doing fine. I like having her.'

And so Suzy swam the Channel for a bit.

But she began to get very tired and she was afraid of being left behind. The man kept having to wait for her to catch up.

'Maisie, pick her up,' Jim said at last. 'She's slowing me down.'

Suzy felt herself being scooped up out of the water.

'Chez-moi!' she wailed furiously. She ran to the edge of the boat, dived in and started swimming again.

Jim nearly choked. It is very difficult to laugh when you are swimming. Maisie scooped up Suzy once again and this time she trapped her under a lobster pot at the bottom of the boat.

'She seems to be as silly about wanting to swim the Channel as you are!' Maisie said.

Suzy didn't like the lobster pot, but she was so exhausted that she hadn't the energy to fight it for long. She lay down and sulked.

'That's better,' Maisie said. 'You're much too small to swim such a long way. You stay here with me.' She took her out and dried her and wrapped her in a warm towel, keeping a firm hold on her.

It dawned on Suzy at last that the boat was following the swimmer. So she *was* going to France, and really it was much easier to go there on Maisie's lap than by swimming. She settled down happily.

Maisie looked at her watch. 'You're making good time, Jim,' she called out. 'We should catch the tide.'

But she spoke too soon. The wind started to get up and the sea got rougher and rougher. Jim found it more and more difficult to move forward. In the end it got so bad that he was hardly moving at all, and Maisie had to turn off the boat's engine to stay with him. The boat began to be tossed about, too, as the waves got bigger and bigger, and Maisie put Suzy back under the lobster pot to keep her safe.

Jim struggled on for a bit, but it was no good. He would have missed the tide now anyway.

Suzy couldn't believe it when she saw him being helped into the boat, and when the boat turned round and headed back for England it was the last straw.

'Chez-moi!' she cried, heartbroken. 'Chez-moi!'

'I'm sorry, Pussy,' said Jim. 'I thought you were going to bring me luck, but it seems that I was wrong. Never mind. I'll try again tomorrow.'

Suzy only knew that she wasn't going home to France.

'Chez-moi!'

'There, she's telling me she's sorry,' said Jim. He put on a thick sweater and some trousers and had a cup of coffee. Now that

the engine was full on, the boat wasn't toss-
ing nearly so much, so Jim took Suzy out of
the lobster pot and she rode the rest of the
way back to England on his lap. He made a
great fuss of her.

'She had plenty of guts, this little one,' he
said to Maisie. 'Maybe she couldn't swim the
Channel, but I bet she could swim the
Thames. I can see it now in *The Guinness Book
of Records:* "First cat to swim the Thames in
the record-breaking time of five minutes".
What about that, Pussy cat?' He stroked
Suzy's ears. Suzy purred and then fell fast
asleep.

When she woke up they were back at the
pier.

'Hard luck, Jim,' people were saying. 'Are
you going to try again?'

'Tomorrow if the weather's kind,' he said.

'I think I'll take my lucky cat with me.' He looked around. 'Oh, where is she?'

Suzy had slipped away in the crowd and run home to Auntie Jo.

'Pussy cat, Pussy cat, where have you been?' said Biff.

'Swimming the Channel by the look of her!' Auntie Jo said. 'Oh, Pussy cat, you are a shocker.'

'Shocker!' said Biff. 'Shocker! Clever Biff.'

Auntie Jo dried Suzy again and gave her her dinner – a piece of chicken. Suzy ate it all up. It wasn't fish, but it was very good.

'Merci,' she said, cleaning her whiskers.

'Merci,' said Biff, 'shocker!'

And Suzy purred.

But she did miss Gaby stroking her the wrong way.

6 Suzy nearly goes under

The next morning Suzy waited patiently in the hall by the door while Auntie Jo speared her hat to her bun. It was a different hat today – a flowery one. Auntie Jo saw Suzy reflected in the glass.

'Now, Pussy cat,' she said. 'It's no good you waiting there today. It's Sunday – I'm going to Church. I'm not taking you with me.'

But of course, she was. Suzy settled herself into the basket the minute Auntie Jo had

wheeled out her tricycle, and nothing Auntie
Jo said or did would move her.

'All right,' said Auntie Jo at last. 'Come –
but you'll have to wait outside during the
service.'

'Chez-moi!' replied Suzy, quite happy.

Auntie Jo went a different way today,
turning out of the town. The Church was at
the top of a hill and Auntie Jo had to get off
and push the tricycle for the last bit. Suzy
didn't mind. She sat up in the basket and
looked about her. The church was on a headland – a piece of land which stuck out into the
sea – and Suzy could see into the bay on the
other side. There were ships there, big
ships!

The moment Auntie Jo parked the tricycle by the church porch Suzy was off like a
rocket over the headland.

'Oh dear,' said Auntie Jo. 'I hope she doesn't go down to the sea again.'

Suzy took a short cut down a cliff path, streaked across the sand and up some steps to a big quay. There was a smart motor-boat decorated with flags just about to leave the jetty. Suzy jumped neatly down and settled herself behind a pile of rope.

With a roar the motor-boat shot off across the bay, a plume of white foam behind it. There were a lot of men in uniform on board, including an Admiral, but of course Suzy didn't notice that. All she knew was that they were going towards France!

Or were they? The boat was drawing up alongside a very odd sausage-shaped ship. Oh well, perhaps she'd still get there.

Suzy joined the end of the procession that was going aboard the ship. The sailors already on the ship were all lined up ready to be inspected by the Admiral. Someone was making an awful piping noise on a funny kind of whistle.

The Admiral began to strut importantly between the lines of men. Suzy, who was determined not to be left behind, trotted importantly behind him, for all the world as if inspecting the fleet was something she did every day of her life. Eyes front, tail erect, her football-sock paws lifting neatly as she stepped along the deck, Suzy was almost as dignified

as the Admiral himself – and he had all his gold braid to help him!

The men were trying hard not to grin; it was not often that they had to stand to attention to be inspected by a small tabby cat!

By the end of the inspection Suzy was beginning to feel a little impatient. What was all this walking about for? Why didn't they get on with it and make for France?

Well, they did begin to get on with something. The Admiral went back to his motorboat to be taken ashore. Suzy didn't want *that* so she ran and hid behind a sort of tower.

When the Admiral's boat had gone, the ship's Captain gave the order: 'Make ready to submerge!' Of course, Suzy didn't know what that meant.

The sailors rushed about slamming doors and hatches. Suddenly Suzy was the only one left on top of the ship. The men had all disappeared.

Well, as long as she got to France, Suzy didn't mind having a lonely ride.

But what was happening? The ship was sinking! Suzy watched with horror as the ship went down, down and the water came up, up towards her. Soon the main part of the ship had completely disappeared and although Suzy had scrambled to the top of the tower thing, that was sinking too!

Poor Suzy. She clung to the last bit sticking out of the top and stared at the empty sea around her. The shore was terribly far away.

Inside the submarine the Captain took a last look through the periscope.

'Funny!' he said. 'I can't see a thing. There seems to be something blocking it.'

'Let's have a look,' said the First Officer.

'Good heavens! The Admiral's moggy! We'll have to surface.'

'Moggy?' the Captain said. 'What is a . . . ?'

'Cat,' said the First Officer. 'You remember; the one that inspected us. I thought he would have taken her ashore with him. Careless chap. Oh well. Surface?'

'Yes,' sighed the Captain. 'Someone will have to take her ashore.'

So Suzy found herself slowly rising as the ship came to the top of the water again. It *was* a relief! But what were they up to? It really was a most peculiar ship, sinking and un-sinking itself like this. Suzy didn't like it at all.

So she wasn't too upset when a sailor picked her off the conning-tower and took her into a rubber dinghy. It had an outboard motor and they were soon back at the quay.

Suzy had leapt out and was nearly halfway back to Auntie Jo's house before the sailor had had time to secure the dinghy to the harbour wall.

'I was afraid you were lost at sea,' said Auntie Jo when Suzy walked in. 'I nearly cried in Church when we sang a hymn about "those in peril on the sea".' She sang the last bit in a quavery voice. Biff sang it after her in an even more quavery voice.

'For those in peril on the sea. Clever Biff.'

'Oh you are a clever Biff,' said Auntie Jo.

'On the sea. On the sea. Clever Biff. On the sea.' Biff liked singing.

Auntie Jo put a saucer down for Suzy, who had nearly been in peril *under* the sea. It was chicken giblets. It wasn't fish, but it was very good. Suzy ate it all up.

'Merci,' she said, cleaning her whiskers.

151

'You have got a funny miaow,' Auntie Jo said.

'Merci,' said Biff, and then he began to sing. 'On the sea. On the sea. Clever Biff. On the sea.'

Auntie Jo and Suzy were just a little tired of that hymn by bed-time.

Before she went upstairs, Auntie Jo stroked Suzy 'good night'.

Suzy purred.

But she did miss Gaby stroking her the wrong way.

7 *Home by car?*

The next morning Auntie Jo got out her tricycle as usual. Suzy popped into the basket, but then jumped out again and went back into the house. She felt that she ought to say goodbye to Biff because she was *sure* that she would get home to France today.

'Au revoir,' she said, which is French for 'goodbye'.

Biff cocked his head to one side.

'Clever Biff!' said Biff. 'Hello, Auntie Jo.'

Suzy felt that he hadn't got it quite right. When you say goodbye to somebody they usually say goodbye back to you. So she tried again.

'Au revoir.'

This time Biff got it. 'Au revoir!' he said. 'Clever Biff. Au revoir.'

Suzy ran out and was only just in time to catch Auntie Jo, who was already out of the gate.

'I thought you had decided not to come today,' Auntie Jo said as she stopped for Suzy to hop in.

'Chez-moi,' said Suzy.

'You have got a funny miaow,' Auntie Jo said.

They pedalled off down to the shops on the sea-front. Auntie Jo parked the tricycle outside the baker's shop. As she got down from the saddle she turned to Suzy who was poised to jump out of the basket.

'I wonder where you are off to this time?' she said. 'Well, I suppose we will see you at supper,' and she went into the baker's shop.

Suzy jumped down and hurried across the road. She had just spotted something familiar on the other side. It was a French sailor with a bobble on his cap! A French sailor might lead her to a French ship. Suzy began to follow him along the pavement.

The sailor was walking very fast; Suzy had to keep running to keep up with him. They seemed to be going a very long way. After a while the pavement became more crowded and the traffic going past them got heavier and noisier. Suzy realized that they were coming to a big port. She could see cranes and wharves and the masts and funnels of ships.

Ships! Suzy kept as close to her sailor as she could. Oh, surely he would lead her to a French ship!

Poor Suzy. He didn't lead her to a French ship. She lost him altogether for he turned into a large building and disappeared. Suzy tried to follow him, but there was a swing door, and when she tried to go through, it just swung her right round and back on to the step again! She tried again and the same thing happened.

Oh, well. She didn't need the sailor now. He had led her to a port. One of those ships *must* be going to France.

Suzy trotted along a wide road towards the quays where the ships were. There were lots of cars going the same way. One of them drew up at the kerb near Suzy and the driver called out to a man in uniform.

'Is this the way for the ferry to France?'

'That's right, sir. Just keep straight ahead,' said the man.

France! Suzy must stay with this car. As the car moved off again she began to run. It was much harder than following the sailor – Suzy ran and ran until her paws ached.

She was almost giving up when the car slowed to a halt. There was a queue of cars waiting to board the ferry. Suzy had not expected to go home to France by car, but it looked as if that was what she was going to have to do. She ran along the queue looking for a car that she could get inside without being noticed.

She found the very one. The family it belonged to had brought so much luggage that the boot would not shut properly and was tied half-open with rope. This left room for Suzy to nose her way in between a suit-case and a deckchair and find a nice little space where she could curl up. The family in the car behind might have noticed her, but luckily they were busy looking at a map of France to see where they would have to go when they got to the other side of the Channel.

Suzy's car moved slowly forwards. Suddenly there was a great clanking as they went down the ramp and into the hold of the ship. It was dark down there, but there were some lights on. Suzy kept very still, a bit frightened by all the banging and clanging as people got out and slammed their car doors. There were cars behind and cars in front and cars on each side. The slams echoed round the metal sides of the ship.

Suzy's family got out of the car and disappeared through a little door in the side where everybody else was going.

At last it was quiet. Suzy peeped out. There was nobody about. She squeezed between a couple of cars and made for the door that her family had gone through.

But there was a new noise. Suzy stopped and listened. It was the ship's engines. They were off!

Suzy hurried on up some steep stairs and came out into a corridor. This led into a big room full of people sitting at tables and eating. Suzy thought it was a very funny ship – more like a house. Then she saw some more stairs. Could there be bedrooms up there? Suzy climbed up and came out on deck into the sunlight.

There was sea all around them. Suzy ran to the rail that went round the side of the ship and then along it to the stern at the back. She could see England disappearing behind them!

She ran down the other side to the very front of the ship, the bows, and found herself a piece of curled-up rope to sit on.

Suzy sat there, her eyes set towards France.

She was going home at last.

8   Home at last

There was Suzy, sitting like a figure-head in the bows of the ship, getting nearer to France every minute.

A little girl came and sat with her. 'Are you the ship's cat?' she asked.

'Chez-moi!' said Suzy.

'You do have a funny miaow,' said the little girl. 'Granny, look. I've found the ship's cat, and she's got such a funny miaow. You listen.'

Suzy didn't say anything else. She had explained where she was going.

'Perhaps she'd like a bit of sardine sand-
wich,' Granny said.

Suzy did like it. She ate it all up and
cleaned her whiskers.

'Merci,' she said.

'I told you she'd got a funny miaow,' the
little girl said to her granny.

Lots of other children came and talked to
Suzy, but she didn't move from her position
in the bows, which was the nearest she could
get to France.

It seemed a very long time, but at last a
thin line of land appeared ahead of them.

'Look! Look! There's France!' the little
girl shouted, pointing.

France! Suzy could hardly believe it. Soon
she would be home.

Just then a sailor came along – and he saw
Suzy.

'What's that cat doing there?' he said.

'It's the ship's cat,' said the little girl. 'Didn't you know?'

'No, I didn't,' the sailor said. 'We haven't got a ship's cat. She's a stowaway.'

He reached forward and made a grab at Suzy. Suzy dodged him. He didn't look friendly at all. He wasn't.

He chased her all around the ship – down the stairs, along corridors, through the dining-room, past the shop and back up on deck again.

Soon all the children began to join in. They thought it was a wonderful game.

Poor Suzy. She was so near home. Nothing must stop her now. She must hide, but where? Anyway, the mob of laughing, shouting children was too close behind her.

Then she saw the mast. She ran up it like

a squirrel and clung at the very top. Everyone stopped and looked up. No one could reach her.

'I'll get her down,' said the puffing sailor. He went off to fetch a ladder.

Suzy stared around her desperately. There was France getting nearer and nearer – France and home.

Then she saw something else. In the sea ahead of them was a French fishing boat.

And on the deck were four little boys like steps.

It was Suzy's family! It must be.

'Out of the way there!' said the sailor, clearing the children from the foot of the mast. He had come back with a ladder.

But Suzy didn't notice. She leapt straight over his head on to the deck, ran to the rail – and dived!

'Oooooh!' said everybody watching.

'She'll drown!' cried the little girl. 'Somebody save her! Quick!'

But Suzy didn't drown. She seemed to go a very, very long way down into the green water, and then she paddled hard with her little paws and came up to the surface like a cork.

She began to swim. The ship's side towered above her, with a row of faces along the rail. Suzy couldn't see the fishing boat any more because of the waves, but she swam towards the place where she had seen it last.

The little girl waved her arms madly at the boys on the fishing boat and pointed down to Suzy.

'Cat overboard!' she shouted.

The other children joined her: 'Cat overboard!'

The little French boys did not understand, but they saw that the children were pointing to something in the sea. They got their father to turn towards it.

At last there was a calm stretch of water between two waves and the boys spotted something moving there. In a few seconds Suzy was scooped out of the sea with a bucket.

The ferry was already some way away, but they could hear the children cheering because Suzy was safe, and see them waving goodbye.

Suzy was more than safe – she was very, very happy. She sat there in the bucket purring like a ship's engine.

'It's a cat!' said Pierre. 'A swimming cat!'

'Stripey,' said Henri.

'With football socks,' said Paul.

'It's Suzy!' said Gaby, lifting her tenderly out of the bucket and holding her close. 'I knew she would come back.'

That evening, in England, Auntie Jo was getting worried. No Suzy.

'I wonder where she is?' she said aloud. 'She's never missed her dinner before.'

'Shocker!' said Biff. 'Hello, Auntie Jo. Au revoir!'

'What did you say?' Auntie Jo said.

'Clever Biff. Au revoir. Au revoir.'

'Now where did you learn that?' said Auntie Jo. 'I've not taught you that. Of course, she did have a funny miaow. I wonder. . . .'

And the French cat that Auntie Jo was wondering about? She was so full of fish that she could hardly move. She was on the rug in the boys' bedroom in France, being watched by four pairs of shining eyes. She was purring and purring as though she would never stop. Gaby was stroking her the wrong way!

Suzy was home at last.

Also by Jill Tomlinson

The Aardvark Who Wasn't Sure

Pim is a baby aardvark. His mother has told him so. But Pim still isn't quite sure, because he doesn't seem to be able to do any of the things that other aardvarks can do. As he grows up, however, Pim finds out that these things have to be learned, sometimes from his mother and sometimes from the other creatures he meets. As time goes on, he becomes increasingly sure that he really is an aardvark after all!

Jill Tomlinson

The Otter Who Wanted To Know

Pat is a young sea otter who never stops
asking questions – although she doesn't
always listen to the answers!

Life can be dangerous for a young otter
though, and Pat quickly learns how to deal
with hungry sharks and sudden storms.
Then, one day, Pat has a Great Adventure –
and it is so exciting that she almost forgets to
ask any questions!

Jill Tomlinson

Penguin's Progress

Otto is a penguin chick and he lives with lots of other penguins in the ice and snow of Antarctica, at the bottom of the world.

But Otto is different from all the other chicks he knows because he is "first chick", the first penguin born that year, so it's his job to look after all the younger ones as they grow up. But nobody has told him what "growing up" means, and life is both confusing and exciting for Otto as he wonders what will happen next!